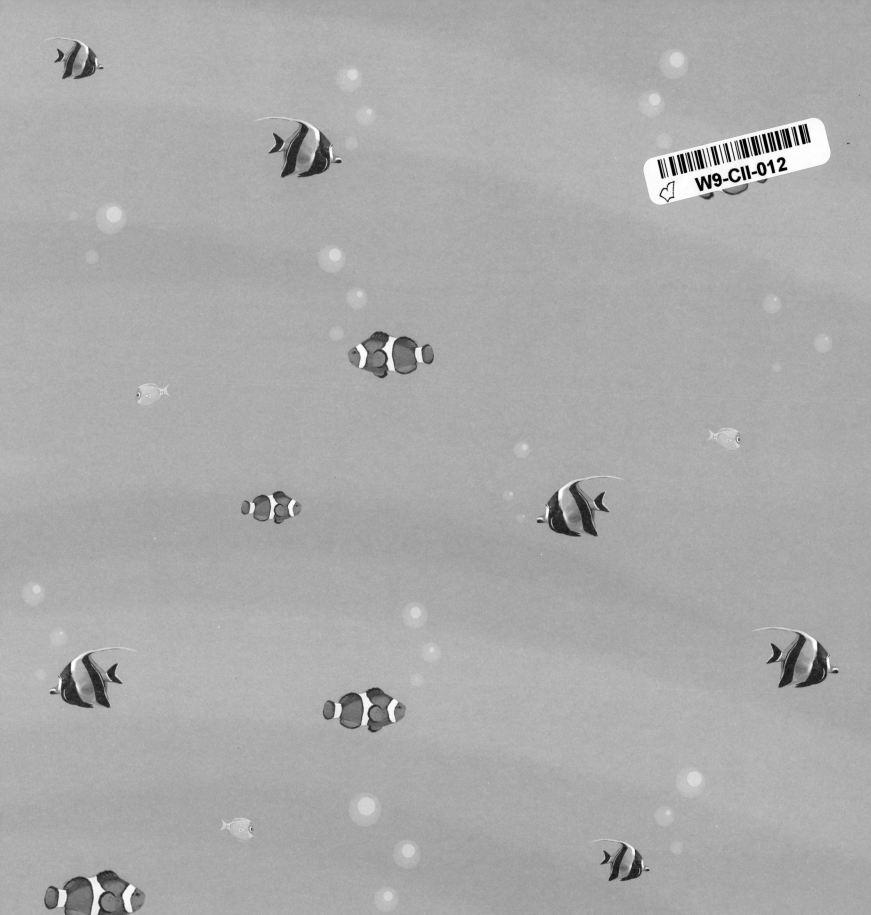

A DOLPHIN'S WISH

How YOU Can Help Make a Difference and Save Our Oceans

Written by Trevor McCurdie • Illustrated by Cinzia Battistel

My Dad can tell a wicked story

of **fearsome** sharks and brave John Dory.

He tells me tales of **mighty** whales

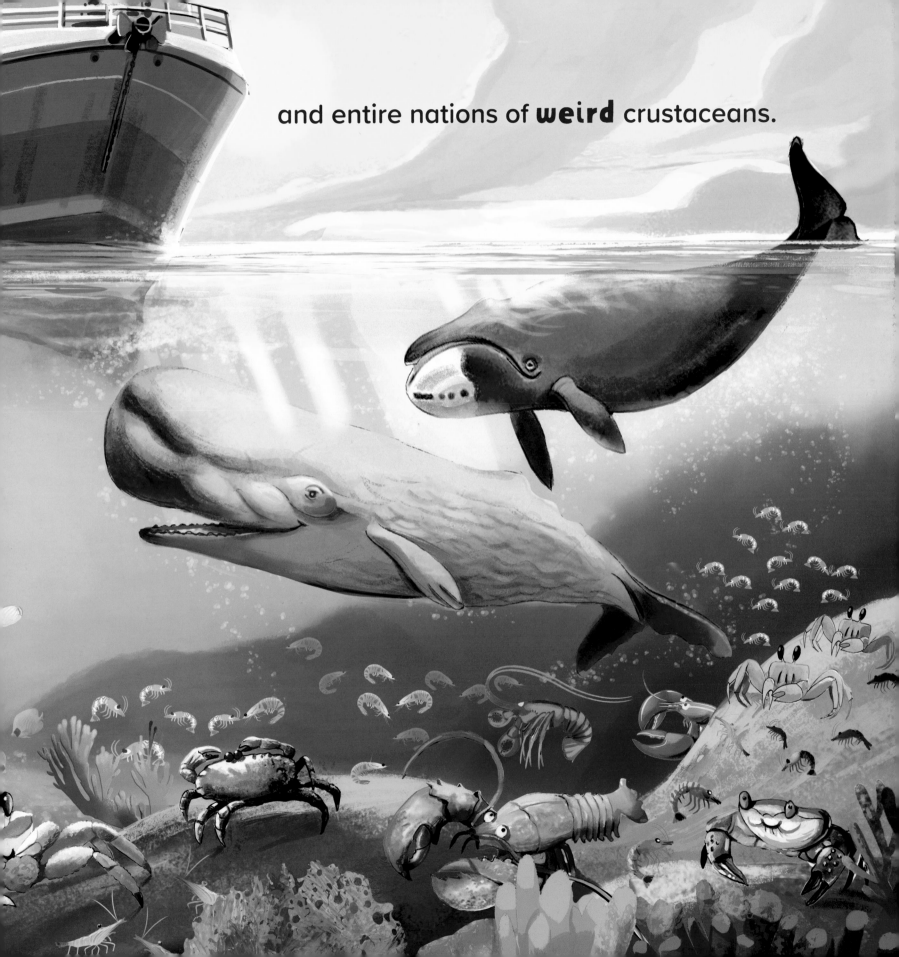

and entire nations of **weird** crustaceans.

But now as I sit upon his fin,
there's a tear in his eye as we begin.
For tonight, Dad's story is not fantastic,
but instead it's a warning about evil **plastic**.

This is a story I've never heard.

"Is plastic a **fish?**

Or maybe a **bird?**

Is *it* **bigger** than me and ever so **scary?**

Or small and cute like the **magic** fish fairy?"

"It's all of these things and much, much more!
It's like no danger we've faced before.
It can **swallow** you whole, and **trap** you inside.
Or get in your tummy, stay there and **hide**."

"I don't like this story, it's way too **creepy!**
I'm just scared, and not at all sleepy."

"I know, I'm sorry, my precious one,
for your life has only just begun.
And already there's things that you must know
because we want to see you **grow** and **grow**."

"Me too, Dad! I want to be
the **biggest** dolphin in the sea!

I'll help the old and the babies, too.
I want to be...**just like you**."

"And that's just what Mom and I wish
for you, the whales, and all the fish.
But we need our rivers and the sea
to be **clean** and **blue** like they used to be."

"We need those creatures
with **nets** and **hooks**

to come down here and take a look."

"Then they'd see that *the* litter they drop is plastic rain and it's **got to stop!**"

"Come on, Dad, let's not end there.
We have to hope the **children care**.
There's lots of things that they can do
to make our ocean **just like new**."

How YOU can help SAVE OUR OCEANS

How does plastic get into our oceans?

Waste from factories that make plastic.

Nets and other lost fishing equipment.

Litter dropped in towns and cities.

Trash we flush down the toilet.

THE SEA STARTS HERE

DON'T LITTER

Garbage left on beaches and thrown into our rivers.

How much plastic leaks into our oceans?

Enough plastic is thrown away each year to circle the Earth **4** times.

One garbage truck of plastic is being dumped into our oceans **EVERY MINUTE.**

By **2050**, there could be more plastic in the ocean than fish.

We produce over
300
million tons of plastic every year.

That's the same weight as
900
Empire State Buildings.

Half of this is only used once before it's dumped!

How does plastic hurt our oceans?

Birds and sea life fill up their tummies with plastic—leaving no room for real food.

The Great Pacific Garbage Patch is a floating island made of trash. It is twice the size of Texas and is getting bigger!

It contains **88,000** tons of plastic.

Smaller creatures get caught up in plastic bags and fishing nets.

That's the same weight as **500** jumbo jets!

Ocean plants produce 50% of the oxygen we breathe. Plastic rain can destroy them!

How long until the garbage disappears?

Toilet paper 1 month	Balloons 6 months	Plastic straw 200 years	Soda can 200 years	Plastic Toothbrush 500 years	Fishing line 600 years	Plastic bag 20–1000 years	Plastic bottle 450–1000 years

Use these words to teach friends about pollution.

Ecosystem
A group of animals and the environment they live in. Plastic trash pollutes ecosystems.

Food Chain
The order in which living things eat one another to get food in their environment. They can end up eating plastic.

Garbage Patches
Huge areas in the ocean formed by gyres pulling trash together.

Biodegradable
Things that slowly disappear on their own, like a leaf or an apple core, without hurting the environment.

Gyre
A gigantic ocean current that swirls in a circle.

Microbeads
Tiny plastic pellets that are smaller than a grain of sand.

Microplastics
Pieces of plastic (smaller than your tiniest fingernail) that can be used to make other plastic things.

Pollution
Anything that is put into the air, land, or water that hurts the environment.

Ghost Nets
Nets that have been forgotten or lost by fishing activity. Sea creatures easily get caught up and hurt in them.

Single-Use Plastic
Something made of plastic that is only used once before it's thrown away.

THIS HAS TO STOP!

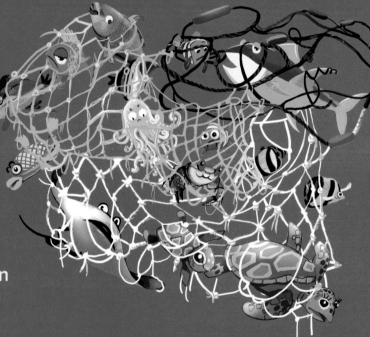

For my pod: Sarah,
Ruby, and Leo.
– TM

For all those who
love the planet.
– CB

Written by Trevor McCurdie
Illustrated by Cinzia Battistel
Designed by Ryan Dunn

Copyright © Hometown World Ltd 2019

Published by Sourcebooks eXplore, an imprint of Sourcebooks Kids
P.O. Box 4410, Naperville, Illinois 60567-4410
(630) 961-3900
sourcebookskids.com

Source of Production: Shenzhen Wing King Tong Paper Products Co. Ltd.,
Shenzhen, Guangdong Province, China
Date of Production: November 2019
Run Number: 5016566
Printed and bound in China.
WKT 10 9 8 7 6 5 4 3 2 1

FSC
www.fsc.org

MIX
Paper from
responsible sources
FSC® C010256

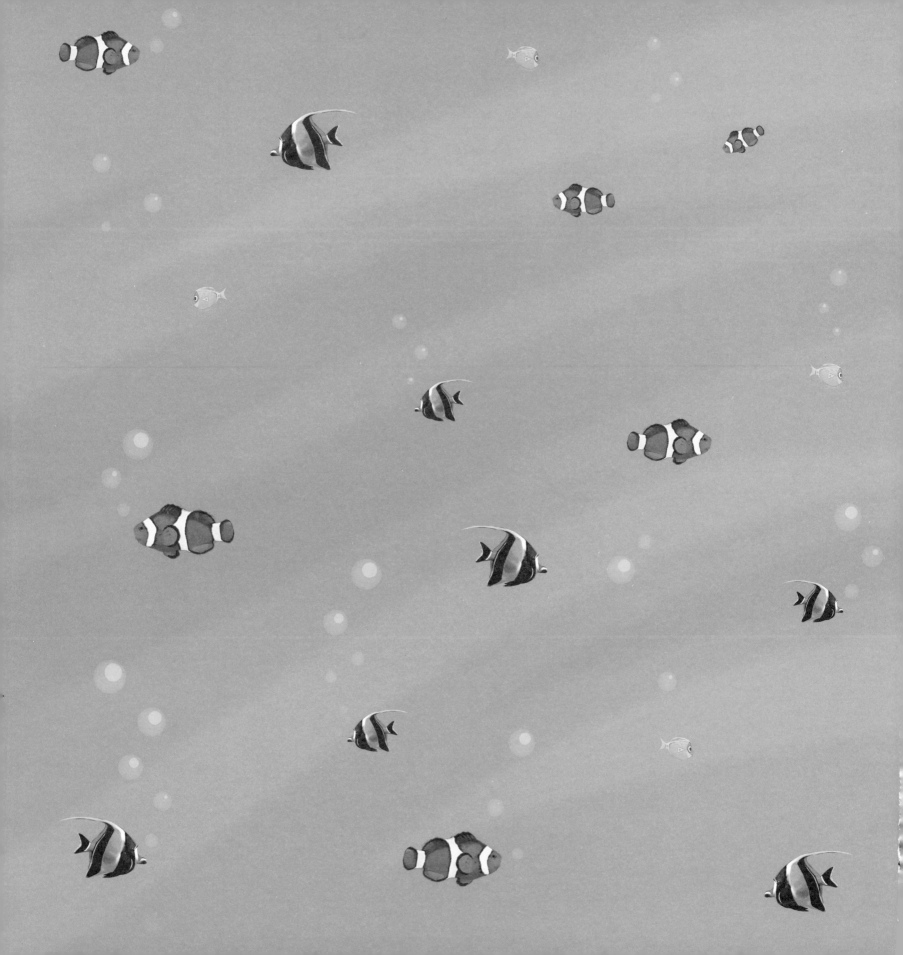